CATCH THAT KID

Adapted by Suzanne Weyn

Based on the screenplay
by Michael Brandt & Derek Haas

SCHOLASTIC INC.

New York   Toronto   London   Auckland   Sydney

Mexico City   New Delhi   Hong Kong   Buenos Aires

ISBN 0-439-58811-1

12 11 10 9 8 7 6 5 4 3 2   4 5 6 7 8 9/0

Printed in the U.S.A.
First printing, March 2004

Chapter 1

Maddy

Ring! My cell phone suddenly burst into song. I wasn't expecting it, and I jumped.

Bad move — especially since I was hanging off the side of a 50-foot water tower! I began falling fast.

Down!

Down!

I slammed against the tower I'd just climbed and continued to fall even farther.

Snap!

My safety line tightened and held tight. Lucky thing! I hung there at the end of the rope. My heart was banging like a jackhammer, but I was okay.

And my cell phone was still playing its little song. I quickly unclipped it from my climbing belt and checked my caller ID. "Hi, Mom," I answered, trying to make my voice sound as casual as I could.

"What are you doing, Madeline?" she demanded suspiciously. Why did she think I was doing something I shouldn't be doing? How could she possibly know that I was climbing up the side of a huge water tower after she'd told me not to? What strange powers did moms have that enabled them to know stuff like that?

I hung there, my legs kicking the air. High up as I was, I could look out and see the setting sun turning all the rooftops pink and yellow. "Homework," I replied. "I'm just doing my homework."

Okay, so it wasn't exactly true. I didn't want to upset her.

"Are you climbing?" she asked. *How* did she know? I mean, how could she possibly know?

"No, Mom," I lied. There was no sense making her worry. This security job she was working on at the bank was not going well, and she was very stressed. I figured that a white lie was better than getting her all upset.

Mom has her own business setting up security systems for companies and banks. She takes her work very seriously, and she sometimes works a lot of hours. Tonight was one of those nights.

"I have to work late," she explained, "so I'm going to need you to . . ."

". . . pick up Max from day care," I completed her sentence. It was the fifth day that week I'd had to go get my baby brother because Mom was working late.

"It won't be forever, sweetie, just until I finish this project," she said.

Sure, sure, I thought. It would be just until she finished this project and started the next one. Though, to be fair, it did seem that this project at the Lyons World Bank was taking longer than usual.

"So, you'll get Max?" she asked again.

"If I have to," I said. Max is an okay kid, but I'm twelve, and I was on break. Didn't I deserve to have some fun? I didn't want to spend my entire vacation baby-sitting.

I sighed. There was no way I could get out of it. I guess Mom didn't like being stuck at work any more than I liked baby-sitting. "Sure," I agreed. "I'll come right down."

"Down?" she asked.

"Over," I corrected myself quickly, trying to cover up. "You know what I mean."

She seemed to believe me. "I'll see you later," she said.

I flipped my phone closed and reattached it to my climbing belt. I wasn't too far from the ground now. I unclipped myself from the safety line and dropped down.

I'd just had a close call, but it wouldn't stop me from climbing the tower again. Each time I climbed it, I marked how high I'd climbed and the date that I'd done it. My goal was to some-day reach the top. I know that a water tower isn't Mount Everest, but it was a beginning.

Climbing was in my blood. My dad was an awesome mountain climber, and he'd taught me everything he knew. Checking my trail watch, I saw that I had enough time to go see him at work before I had to go and get Max. It was even on the way to the day-care center. So I decided to head for the go-cart track.

Chapter 2

Gus

The four other guys in our pit crew held up the go-cart while I worked fast under the cart, trying to get the tire bolted back on. The driver paced back and forth beside me. He was about to throw a total fit if I didn't get the cart back on the track in the next second. "Hey, I'm losing this race because of you!" he yelled down at me.

Turning on my side, I glanced up at him. He reminded me of Darth Vader with that bulky, black helmet he wore. There was no doubt — Chad was a scary guy.

Working as fast as I could, I twisted the lug nut hard with my wrench. This driver was a terror, and I didn't want to make him any angrier than he was already.

"I can't believe Mom made me use you as my lead mechanic!" he screamed. That's right; this hysterical maniac was my own 16-year-old brother, Chad. If I didn't get him back on the track instantly, there would be no escaping him, even when I went home.

"Done!" I announced giving the lug nut a last turn.

"You'd better pray this works," Chad snarled at me as he climbed into the go-cart. He hit the gas and shot off onto the track. The cart turboed past three other carts. Chad was heading for the lead spot.

Whew! Chad was doing great out there, so at least he wouldn't torment me tonight after we got home.

And then it happened. . . .

Chad hit the first turn in the track, and the cart began to spit out a plume of gray smoke. It shuddered to a stop as the two back wheels came loose and rolled off down the track.

I swallowed hard as I suddenly realized that I still held four metal lug nuts in my right hand. They weren't supposed to be in my hand! They were supposed to be holding the wheels on the go-cart! Somehow I'd forgotten to fasten them back on the wheels — which was why those wheels were now rolling down the track without the rest of the go-cart. "Uh-oh," I murmured.

Chad's angry shouts reached me loud and clear even though they came from inside his Darth Vader helmet. "I'm going to get you, you moron! You'd better run because I'm going to destroy you!"

The four other pit crew guys raced out onto the track to help him. One of them nudged me on the head as he passed. "Good job, dork," he said.

Chad was beyond furious, and he was headed straight for me. "I'm going to kill you!" he screamed, and I had no doubt that he meant it.

I made a run for it, but Chad was next to me in a second. I backtracked to the tool cart as Chad chased me around it. I kept the tool cart between us for a few minutes, but then Chad faked left before he lunged right. The next thing I knew, I was in a full headlock.

"Ow! Ow! Ow!" I shouted. I twisted and squirmed until I was looking up at Chad. He squeezed tighter. Was every big brother as vicious as mine? Chad was always doing stuff like this to me, but I never seemed to get used to it. "Let me go!" I squealed.

Then another face came into view.

"Hi," I squeaked to Maddy Philips, who was looking down at me. Maddy's my next-door neighbor, and she's really cute. It was more than a little humiliating to see her under these circumstances.

"Why don't you pick on someone your own size?" she said to Chad.

"Climber girl," Chad sneered at her. He meant it as an insult, but that just shows you how dumb Chad is. Maddy is proud of being a climber, and she should be. The way she climbs is awesome.

"I thought once you got to junior high, you'd stop hanging out with losers," Chad said to Maddy. He sneered at me in case I didn't realize that *I* was the loser he was talking about.

Maddy's face lit up with that great smile she has. "I guess you were wrong," she said.

That confused Chad, which isn't too hard to do. While he tried to figure out what she meant, I was able to wriggle out of his grip. Chad is tough, but fortunately, it's easy to out think him.

I noticed a scrawny-looking kid walking toward us. I should have known he'd show up. Austin always seems to appear whenever Maddy's around.

"Look, it's loser number three," Chad said, jerking his head toward Austin. I didn't think the guy was a loser, but I wasn't exactly glad to see him, either.

Austin and I weren't friends — far from it. There was a simple reason why. We both wanted to go out with Maddy. Every time I tried to talk to Maddy, though, Austin somehow was there — just like right then. The guy had an amazing talent for turning up whenever I had a chance to spend time alone with her.

Of course Austin didn't just *happen* to be there. He has zero interest in go-carts. Once I saw him try to drive a go-cart, and he spun it in a circle until he got so dizzy he just fell out. No, he only comes because Maddy's dad, Tom, owns the track. Maddy's tight with her dad and so she comes here a lot. And wherever Maddy is, that's where you'll find Austin. What a sap!

Sure I like Maddy, but I don't go trailing her around like Austin does. I'm really crazy for go-carts. I love everything about them.

"You guys want to come over?" Maddy offered. "We're going to barbecue."

"Definitely," I answered.

That geek Austin shouted out "Definitely" at the same time as me. How embarrassing! What a dweeb! I shot him my meanest look, and he gave me the same icy stare right back.

Maddy started to walk away, but Chad called out to her. "Hey, I don't know if you heard. Bad Chad picked up a shift at your mother's bank. That puts me one step closer to being a cop," Chad said. He was superpumped that he'd gotten this security guard job.

"Don't worry, they won't let 'Bad Chad' carry a weapon. He's just an intern," I added. I knew I'd pay for that remark at home, but I couldn't resist.

"Trainee, butt wad," my brother corrected me.

"Ouch . . . sorry. He's training to be a butt wad," I said. I was on a roll and there was no stopping me. Chad began trying to grab me. I jumped away from him, laughing. "Doing a good job of being a butt wad, too."

"I'm going to brain you!" Chad growled as he grabbed at me. I ran away from him, still laughing.

Was I showing off for Maddy? Definitely.

Was she impressed? I had no idea.

Was Chad going to destroy me? Probably — but he was going to have to catch me first!

Chapter 3

Maddy

I stood next to Austin and watched Gus try to get away from Chad. He dodged around corners, zigzagged, and then backtracked, jumping over tools, small kids, and go-carts. It was pretty cool the way he took on his big brother, even though Chad was sure to pulverize him. At least Gus wasn't a wimp.

"He's so immature, isn't he?" Austin said.

I gave him a look that said, *Yeah, like you're not*. Austin's a good kid — real smart — but I wish he'd let up on Gus. I've been friends with them both ever since I was a little kid. Gus has lived next door, like, forever, and I met Austin in kindergarten. They're my two very best friends. But they have some kind of strange feud going. I don't understand it.

From across the track, I spotted my dad walking in behind the front counter. He was holding a baby. It wasn't Max but some other baby, one I didn't know. I had to find out what was going on. "I'll see you later," I told Austin as I headed toward Dad.

As I got closer to him, I saw a woman come and take the baby from him. "Thank you for watching him, Tom," I heard her say to Dad.

"Anytime," he replied with a smile.

A teenage kid waved to him as he headed out the door. "See ya, Mr. P.!"

Dad waved back. "Great job today, Oliver. I'll see you next week."

Another woman stopped to talk to him on her way out. She held up a book as she spoke. "Tom, you were right. I loved this book."

He nodded. "You can never go wrong with the classics," he said. That was my dad — everybody liked him and he made everybody feel great.

He went to the microphone at the desk. "It's

race time!" he announced. "Hit the gas and kick some butt, all you go-cart fans out there! We're here to have big fun!"

Dad noticed me coming toward him and smiled. "Hey, kiddo! What's up?" he greeted me.

"Mom needs me to pick up Max," I told him.

"Again, huh?" he said. We walked together toward his office. He knew how I felt about having to watch Max. If he hadn't been working at the track, he would have done it. Dad was good like that. He helped Mom a lot when he could. I was glad he had a job where I could spend time with him, like now.

We were nearly to his office when the smile faded from his face, and he grimaced in pain. His whole body tensed, and he leaned against the wall.

"Dad?" I asked, worried. "Are you okay?"

He fished a small bottle of aspirin from his jeans pocket and popped two in his mouth. I'd seen him do this more and more in the last month. I had no idea what could be wrong with him. Normally he was such an athletic, healthy guy. He never complained about aches and pains.

Dad waved his hand to say there was nothing really wrong. After a couple of minutes he relaxed a little. He still looked pale, though, and it worried me.

He looked at me and frowned. "Is that a new style the kids are sporting?" he asked.

Oops! I'd totally forgotten that I still had on my climbing harness. "Dad, don't freak out," I said.

"Madeline, when do I ever freak out?" he asked. That was true. Dad was almost always cool. I never saw him get angry or upset about anything. But I knew he didn't want me climbing any more than Mom did. "There are a thousand other sports that don't involve falling a hundred feet to your death," he said. "Mom and I just don't want anything to happen to you."

He'd said this so many times, but I didn't believe him. Sure, I believed he didn't want me to get hurt. But I also knew that he understood why I loved to climb so much — why I needed to climb. "You told me that standing on Mount Everest was the best day of your life," I argued as we entered his small office. I pointed to the framed photo he kept on the wall. It showed him standing on top of the mountain, which just happens to be the highest peak in the entire world! In that picture, he looked windburned and incredibly happy.

"No," he corrected me. "I said it was *one* of the best days of my life."

"What's wrong with me trying to be like you?" I asked him.

"Do we have to discuss this every day?" he asked with a sigh.

We did talk about it a lot. That was because I couldn't accept that they didn't want me climbing. "I'm your daughter," I reminded him. "Climbing is what we do!"

"Well, right now we're not," he said. "You go get Max, and I'll head home to start the barbecue."

"I invited Gus and Austin," I told him. "That's okay, isn't it?"

"Super," he said. I gave him a wave and headed out to go get Max. "Maddy," he called to me when I was nearly to the door. "One more thing."

"What?"

"Take off the climbing vest before Mom gets home."

"Will do," I promised. I looked over to where I'd last seen Gus and Austin, but both of them were gone.

Chapter 4

Austin

I got to Maddy's house before Gus got there. That was pretty amazing considering that he lives right next door. Some guys have all the luck. Maybe he was still running around trying to get away from Chad. I hoped so. I wanted to look my best for the Philipses' barbecue.

When I arrived, Mr. Philips answered the door. "Hi, Austin. Maddy's inside changing Max, but you're just in time to play my new Playstation car racing game with me," he said.

What a great guy! Mr. Philips was probably the coolest dad I knew. We went onto his porch where he'd set up an old TV just for video games. How cool is that?

I have to admit that car racing, even *video* car racing, is not exactly something I excel at. In fact, within seconds, I'd smashed my video sports car into an 18-wheeler truck. At the same time, Mr. Philips raced his video Ferrari under the truck and over the finish line. "Show me da money!" he cheered, holding his arms up in triumph.

"Hey!" I cried. "How come I crashed into the truck but you drove right under it? How'd you do that?"

Mr. Philips got up and stretched. "Press X, Y, and hold R2," he said. Even though I wasn't a fan of car racing, I had to admire the guy's mastery of the video game. Considering he was somebody's *father*, he was pretty awesome.

As Mr. Philips opened the porch door to go out to check his barbecue, a football came flying in. He caught it, which was lucky because if he hadn't, it would have hit me right in the face.

"Mr. P., why can't I throw a spiral?" Gus

whined from outside. I should have known only a goober like Gus would throw a football into someone's front porch.

Mr. Philips tossed the ball back outside to him. "It's not a ball, it's an egg," he told Gus. "You have to hold it as lightly as you would an egg."

Gus followed Mr. Philips to the grill and stood there talking to him. I wasn't going to let him hog this great guy — my future father-in-law! I had loved Maddy ever since kindergarten. I was absolutely positive that someday I would marry her. The idea of having Mr. Philips as my father-in-law was just icing on the cake, the wedding cake, that is.

But here was Gus taking all of Mr. Philips's attention for himself. He was probably trying to win him over so he'd put in a good word with Maddy. I was not about to let *that* happen! So I hurried out to join them.

"Mr. P., can I ask you a serious question?" I heard Gus say as I came up behind him. This sounded interesting.

"Only if you want a serious answer," Mr. Philips replied.

"Do girls like guys who build things with their hands?" Gus asked.

Oh, who could he possibly be talking about? He wouldn't mean himself, Mr. Go-cart-Builder-All-around-Screw-up, would he? It was so obvious I felt like laughing — so I did.

He whirled around and glared at me. He was always shooting me nasty stares, but I didn't care. I fired off a pretty deadly looking glare right back.

"You know the kind of guy I mean," Gus went on talking to Mr. Philips, "handsome, manly types. Or do they go for nerds who read women's magazines and play computer games and stuff?" He stared right at me when he said that last line. What a nimrod! I wasn't about to let him get the last word.

"What he *means*," I said, staring right back at him, "is do women prefer a low-IQ kind of Neanderthal guy who knows a lot about spark plugs or a guy with both sensitivity and a brain?"

Mr. Philips smiled and looked toward the porch. Gus and I looked, too. Maddy was there walking around with Max. I guess all three of us knew what this conversation was really about.

"That's a very difficult question, boys," Mr.

Philips replied after a moment. "But I'm not the person to ask. Hey, Madeline Rose."

No! What was he doing? This could be too humiliating. Gus must have thought so, too. He looked just as sick as I felt. Just a minute ago, I thought Mr. Philips was the greatest guy on earth. Now, suddenly, I was living in dread, fearing his next words. At the same moment, Gus and I both lunged at him and clamped our hands over his mouth.

Maddy came out of the porch and onto the deck with Max in her arms. "Dad, don't call me that," she complained. Then she noticed that we were covering her dad's mouth. "What are you guys doing?" she asked.

"Nothing," I said, taking my hand off Mr. Philips's mouth.

Gus removed his hand and said "nothing" at the exact same time. He was always doing that! It was so embarrassing!

Gus then tried to strike one of his Mr. Cool poses. He leaned into the grill and slapped his hand down right square on it. "Owww!" he howled.

Now *that* was funny! "Smooth," I said before bursting out into hysterical laughter.

"Shut up!" Gus shrieked, shaking his hand in pain.

Mr. Philips grabbed a can of cream soda and poured it over Gus's hand. "Ancient Chinese burn cure," he told him.

Gus winced in pain but calmed down. I checked his palm. He had a nasty grill mark right across it. As much as Gus bugs me, I wouldn't wish that kind of painful burn on anybody. "You're going to have a scar," I said sympathetically.

A big grin spread across Gus's face. A scar was just about the coolest thing to an immature, macho guy like Gus. To tell the truth, I thought scars were pretty wicked, too. All the sympathy I'd felt a second ago disappeared. "Why do you get all the cool stuff?"

Mr. Philips nodded knowingly. "It's true, women love scars. This drives Maddy's mom crazy." He lifted his shirt and showed us a huge scar on his back.

"Whoa!" Gus and I said at the same time. We had to stop doing that! But it *was* an awesome scar.

"You can touch it if you want," Mr. Philips

said. We leaned closer to inspect it. The scar snaked all the way down his spine.

"Is this from when you fell?" I asked. Maddy told me her dad had taken a bad fall when he was climbing Mount Everest. It nearly killed him. He never climbed again.

"Yep," he said, "it was a hundred-foot free fall."

"Wow!" I said. And guess who yelled "wow" at the exact same moment. This was getting ridiculous.

Chapter 5

Maddy

Mom walked out on the deck as the guys were going wild over Dad's scar. She gave me a questioning look, but I just shrugged. It wasn't something I felt I could actually explain.

She took Max from me and nuzzled him. "Hello, my little chicken nugget," she cooed to him. I tried not to mind. After all, Max was only a baby, and I understood he needed Mom's love and attention. But I'd spent the first 11 years of my life as the only child in the family. Since he'd come along, I was feeling a little like . . . well, like old news. Mom was so busy lately, and what little time and energy she had left over was focused on Max.

"C'mon, say Mama," she coaxed Max. "Ma . . . Ma . . ."

Max just stared at her, and Mom sighed. "Why won't you talk? All the other kids are talking."

I knew Mom and Dad were starting to get concerned about Max's lack of speech. When I'd picked him up from day care that evening, I'd thought he was almost about to say my name. I figured that news might cheer Mom up. "Mom," I began, "today he almost said Mad —"

I was interrupted by Mom's beeping cell phone. She checked the Caller ID and gave me an apologetic grimace. I knew that expression. It meant, *This is an important work call and I have to take it.*

Whenever that phone sounded, though, it was *always* something important, something she just had to deal with. To Mom, everything related to her work was always urgent. To be honest, I didn't understand it. I thought we were supposed to be the top priority in her life. It really bugged me when I stopped to think about it.

"Hello, Mr. Brisbane," Mom answered her phone. "Yes. Sorry. I must have just missed your call at the bank. Yes. I know the security system was supposed to be finished yesterday. But I did inform you that due to the age of the building, we might encounter some problems."

Poor Mom. Despite my being annoyed, I also felt sorry for her. This new bank job had been one problem after another. And this Brisbane guy — the bank president — was constantly calling and complaining. It sounded like he was a royal pain to work for.

"I realize you've scheduled the opening of the bank for next Friday night, but that won't give me enough time to test the system," Mom tried to explain to Brisbane. She sat down on a deck chair with Max in her lap. "I wouldn't recommend opening the bank or even having your opening night party until we're sure the system works. Yes, Mr. Brisbane. I understand that you're the boss. I'm only giving you my professional opinion. Yes, sir, see you tomorrow."

She clicked off the call and sighed in frustration. "He's a fool if he opens that bank before I can fix this system," she said. "This is a new bank, but it's in an old building, and we have to run all new wires. He'll hold me responsible if something goes wrong, but it won't be my fault. I wish I'd known how hard this job was going to be when I took it."

"Don't worry, Mom," I said. "You'll get it done. You always do."

"I hope so," she said, sounding unsure. "I've designed a wonderful security system that I'm really proud of. The money is one hundred feet above ground."

"One hundred feet?" I said.

She nodded. "I'd like to see someone try to break into that safe. They could never get that high up. I just need more time to perfect it."

Wow! She'd made a safe that was 100 feet high. I'd love to try to climb that.

"Barbecue!" Dad announced.

That night, I was awakened from a deep sleep by Mom, who burst into my room. "Maddy, you have to take care of Max. I'm going to the hospital with Dad!"

At first I thought I was still dreaming. But I

quickly came fully awake. "Dad? What's wrong with Dad?" I asked, rubbing my eyes.

"He got up to get a snack and collapsed. I've already called the ambulance."

That got me up and moving. I threw a sweatshirt over my PJs and put my bare feet in unlaced sneakers. "I'm coming with you," I said following her down the hall. "I'll get Mrs. Harris next door to take Max."

"Fine," Mom agreed.

A whirling red light told me that the ambulance was here. Mrs. Harris had come over to see what was happening and agreed to stay with Max.

After that everything happened really quickly. The paramedics put Dad in an ambulance. Mom and I followed in the car as they sped him to the hospital. Mom went into the emergency room with him, but I had to stay outside in the waiting room for a long while. It was torture.

Finally, Mom came for me and we went to the hospital room where Dad lay in bed, attached to different tubes and monitors. I was so happy to see that he was awake, his eyes open. "Dad!" I cried as I hurried to his side.

"Hi, honey," he said quietly. It was strange. He didn't turn toward me. He just kept staring at the ceiling. I suddenly realized that he *couldn't* move.

I suddenly went cold with fear. Mom was keeping herself together but she looked pale and scared, too. What could be wrong with Dad? I wondered and suddenly remembered how he'd cringed in pain earlier that day. Did this have something to do with it? I leaned against Dad's bed, weak with fear.

A doctor walked in holding a chart and wearing a white lab jacket over his clothes. I looked at his face closely, trying to tell from his expression if this was serious. "How do you feel, Mr. Philips?" he asked.

"I can't feel my legs," Dad told him. "And I can't seem to roll over."

"What's wrong, doctor?" Mom asked.

The doctor took off his glasses and put down his chart. He seemed to be getting ready to tell us something important and bad. "Mr. Philips is suffering from MND, a rare form of Guillain-Barré syndrome," he said.

"What's that?" Mom asked.

"The nerve path system inside his spine that his brain uses to transmit signals to the major muscle groups has been severed," he said. "The injury probably occurred when he fell on Mount Everest."

"But that was nine years ago." Mom said exactly what I was thinking. How could something that happened so long ago affect him right now? It made no sense to me.

"After he fell, the nerve path slowly weakened," the doctor explained. "He's lucky it's taken this long to paralyze him."

"Lucky?" Mom asked. It sure didn't sound lucky to me, either. As Dad lay there in that hospital bed, the last thing he looked was lucky.

"I simply meant it was fortunate that the injury from the fall didn't paralyze him right away," the doctor said. "But the damage he did to his spine has been like a time bomb waiting to go off all these years."

"Will I be able to move again?" Dad asked.

The doctor hesitated before he answered. "When the spine's involved, there are lots of complications," he said. I didn't like the sound of this, or the very serious expression on the doctor's face. "The blood supply to the brain might be affected."

"So what's that mean?" Dad asked.

The doctor didn't seem to want to answer Dad's question. He just hung his head and seemed to study the floor tiles. It slowly occurred to me what his not answering meant. He didn't want to tell us an awful truth. Dad might die.

Mom understood, too, and her eyes went wide with fear. She looked the way I felt — terrified. "Isn't there some sort of emergency surgery . . . anything?" she asked the doctor.

The doctor considered her question for a long moment before he replied. "There's nothing *we* can do here," he said. "But I did make a call when Mr. Philips came in. There's a private medical facility in Denmark that has done some testing with this kind of injury."

"Okay! Let's go!" Mom said. She looked ready to grab Dad's bed, wheel him right out the door, and hop on the first plane to Denmark.

"Your insurance won't cover it," the doctor told her.

I looked at Mom and then at the doctor and

then back to Mom. What did this thing about the insurance mean? I got the feeling it was a very big deal.

"The operation is considered experimental," the doctor said, "and while it's been highly successful, there isn't enough hard evidence for insurance to —"

"How much?" Mom said, not waiting for him to finish his sentence. "We'll pay for it. How much does it cost?"

The doctor cleared his throat. He didn't look happy. "About a quarter of a million dollars," he said.

Mom stepped back and wobbled on her feet as if she'd just been hit with a bat. She clearly wasn't prepared for that price, but she just had to find a way to pay it — there had to be *some* way!

The doctor turned toward the door. It was as if they had both decided the price was too high and they were giving up. I couldn't let that happen. I grabbed the doctor's sleeve. "We'll pay it! We'll pay it!" I cried. I looked at Mom and begged. "Tell him we'll pay it." Tears ran from my eyes. "Tell him we'll pay it!"

Chapter 6

Gus

I knew something weird was going on when I didn't see Mr. Philips at the track for two days, or Maddy, either. I was hoping they were just on winter break vacation or something. Somehow, deep down, I knew it wasn't that, though. I had this awful feeling something really bad had happened.

Then, on the third afternoon, Maddy showed up at the track. I was so happy and relieved to see her. As I was heading toward her, wouldn't you know it — Austin just *happened* to show up, too. I saw him come in the door right after I noticed Maddy. I don't know how the guy does it!

Austin and I both hurried up to her to ask how she was. That's when she told the two of us what had happened to her dad. I was blown away when she told us what his operation would cost. "A quarter of a million dollars!" I shouted, repeating the amount she told us. "That's two hundred and fifty thousand dollars!" I couldn't even picture what that amount of money would look like.

"What happens if your dad doesn't get the operation?" Austin asked.

Austin thinks he's the sensitive one and I'm just some kind of go-cart—loving goon, but even I had more sensitivity than to ask a question like that!

Maddy just looked down and seemed really sad. I couldn't stand to see her so miserable — or to think of Mr. Philips dying. "We'll go door to door to get donations," I suggested. "Everyone loves your dad. They'll give us money."

Maddy just looked away. I could tell she was about to cry.

"I'll sell my camera," Austin offered. I was impressed. Austin's video camera is his most prized possession. He loves that camera more than anything.

Maddy smiled at him sadly. "It's a quarter of a million dollars, Austin. Do you know how much that is? Mom tried to get a loan from Mr. Brisbane, the president of the bank she's working for, but the creep turned her down. I went with her when she went to see him. He didn't even care that Dad is sick. All he wanted to know was would she be able to get his precious security system working in time for his opening party this Friday. As if Mom hasn't had more important things to think about."

"The guy has no heart," I commented angrily.

"You're right," Maddy said. "He told Mom, 'A bank has no heart, Mrs. Philips. It's just paper in a vault.'"

"That's cold," Austin said.

"But he's the bank president. He could have a heart if he wanted to have one," Maddy argued. "The way he talked about the bank gave me an idea, and I want to talk to you guys about it."

"Anything!" I said.

"Anything!" Austin said at the same time.

We glared at each other. "What's the idea?" I asked.

"Not here," Maddy said. She told us she didn't want to talk about her idea at the track. She asked us to take a walk with her, so we walked until we came to a vacant lot not too far from her house. We sat on a pile of old tires as Maddy started telling us her big idea. By the time she was done, I could easily understand why she didn't want anyone at the track to overhear her.

She wanted us to help her rob a bank! It wasn't just any bank, either. It was the bank her mother was designing the security system for.

"We can't rob a bank!" I said. "It's just not . . . right."

"We'll pay them back," Maddy insisted.

"How?" Austin asked.

"I don't know," Maddy admitted. "But I'll find a way. It'll work."

"Why do you want to rob your mom's bank?" Austin asked.

"Last night, I watched a video I found with Mom's things. It was a guide to operating the entire security system. It tells you everything — and I mean everything — about the operating system, including getting around it and even shutting it off."

I couldn't believe it. Maddy was really serious

about this. "You understand what will happen if we get caught, don't you?" I asked her. "We'll go to jail forever, like until we're twenty-one."

"Nobody will ever suspect us," she said. "Grown-ups treat us like we're five years old. Anyway, how hard could it be? I'll climb to the safe. Gus, you'll take care of transportation, and Austin, you'll take care of the dogs."

Austin suddenly looked a little green. "What dogs?" he asked in his squeaky voice.

"Rottweilers," she told him. "Vicious, killing dogs that patrol the safe." Maddy looked at us with pleading eyes. I could see that she was desperate. "Please. I need you guys."

What kind of guy would I be if I didn't help her? And how could I let down her dad? I stuck my hand out to shake. "For Mr. P.," I said.

With a happy, excited look in her eyes, she put her hand on mine. Then Austin put his hand on both of our hands. "For Mr. Philips," he said.

I guess we had agreed — we were going to rob a bank.

Chapter 7

Maddy

That night, Mom and I went to see Dad at the hospital. "It's strange not being able to move," he said to me. He and I were alone in the room, since Mom had gone downstairs to get Dad a soda. "I've been looking at the same spot on the ceiling for the past three hours," he said.

How awful! I couldn't stand to see him like this. He was trying to be brave, but Mom had just told him she couldn't get the money for the operation. For a moment, I saw him fight back tears, then he struggled to recover from his disappointment. I knew he was trying to be brave for me, and that only made me feel worse.

"You know," he said, "I escaped death on Mount Everest. I think somebody or something protected me back then so that I could come home and get to know you and find out what a great girl you are. Before the accident, I saw you for only a couple of months at a time. After the fall, I bought the track and stayed home. In a way, it was the best thing that could have happened to me."

I knew he was trying to look at the bright side. It was true that I saw more of him after he stopped climbing, but what good was it if I was going to lose him now? It was too much for me to take. "We'll get the money, Dad," I said. "I promise."

I couldn't tell him about my plan. But I was more determined then ever to pull it off. And if it was going to work, I would have to start on it right away.

The next morning, I asked Mom if I could go to work with her at the bank. She agreed, and after we dropped off Max at day care, the two of us drove to the bank. It was truly an awesome-looking place. They had taken a great old building and designed a modern, state-of-the-art bank inside it. Half of it was still under construction, with plastic sheets and scaffolds all around. The other half was perfect. It was all shined up with busy bank employees scurrying around. They all seemed very busy even though the bank still wasn't open for business.

As we walked across the main lobby, I looked up and saw the bank's ceiling. It went way up. There must have been at least eight floors above us. The first level was a sort of balcony, a mezzanine.

I spotted offices up there, but I also saw a very high-tech security desk. "Whoa," I said aloud. It was going to take a lot of planning to get past that. I'd need information, too. Like what it would take to get the guards to leave their posts, even for a second.

My mind was working overtime trying to take in all the details I'd have to remember in order for the robbery to come off without a hitch. I stood there gazing up at the floors of the bank, thinking about my plan.

After a minute, I realized that Mom was gone. I'd been so busy staring up at the security desk that she'd gotten ahead of me. I noticed her waiting for me on the mezzanine.

I hurried up the stairs and caught up. "I love that you wanted to come to work with me, sweetheart, but I need you to keep up," she said as she dug in her bag, searching for her ID card. "I have a lot of work to do."

Mom sounded tired, and I saw that she had dark circles under her eyes. She hadn't slept much since Dad's collapse. Mostly, she just conked out on the couch every night. Working, visiting Dad, and talking to different banks about loans all day was catching up with her. But if my plan worked, she'd finally be able to stop worrying.

"Can I see the safe?" I asked.

"That's just the old safe," she told me as she kept searching in her purse. "The real one is upstairs."

Mom found her ID card and stepped up to the security desk so that the guards could see her. There were a lot of security screens on the wall behind them. Each screen showed various rooms and halls in the bank. They came on and went off at different times.

I couldn't understand why some went on and

others went off. A screen went on right behind the head of one of the guards. It showed a room with three rottweilers pacing up and down. "Hello, doggies," one of the guards said, waving at the screen. That's when I noticed that the guard was Chad, Gus's idiot big brother! It was weird seeing him in a uniform. In my mind, Chad was just my jerky next-door neighbor, Gus's terrible older brother. I couldn't take him seriously as a guard.

At the same moment, Chad realized he was looking at me. "Climber girl," he said.

"And who have we here, Mrs. Philips?" the other guard asked in a phony, sugary-sweet voice. He smiled at me but he had a weasel face, and his smile was completely insincere. His name tag read FERRELL. He seemed like an even bigger idiot than Chad, if such a thing was possible. I couldn't imagine the two of them guarding this bank.

"This is my daughter," Mom told him.

"She'll be safe here with us," Ferrell said to her. I could see he was really full of himself. He acted like he thought he was a secret agent instead of a security guard. I almost felt sorry for Chad. It couldn't be fun having to sit there with

Ferrell. I noticed he had a stick attached to his belt, some kind of electrical weapon. I didn't like the look of it.

Ferrell passed us through the security check and we headed for an elevator. "Your office is upstairs, Mom?" I asked. One of my goals was to learn everything I could about the layout of the bank. By the time I left, I wanted to make sure I knew where I was going.

"Yep. I needed to be near the safe," she explained.

Mom's office is near the safe, I made a mental note. That would be very handy to know.

I gazed up and noticed a camera that seemed to be focused down right on us. Every few minutes a red light under the screen blinked. "Why does it do that?" I asked.

Mom stared at me curiously. "What's with the sudden interest in my work?"

Oops, maybe I was being too obvious. The last thing I needed was for Mom to become suspicious. I remembered how she always seemed to know when I'd been climbing. Once she suspected something was going on, she wasn't easy to fool.

Shrugging, I tried to act casual. "I'm just interested in your work. You know, security is a fascinating field. And I think security cameras are cool."

Mom's eyes narrowed doubtfully, but she seemed to accept my answer. "It's built with a motion detector," she explained. "The guards can't watch all one hundred cameras at once, so when a camera picks up movement, a light comes on and they can see us. Stay still."

We both stood there without moving and stared up at the light. After a few minutes, it went off. I had just learned something very important about the security system. I could make it turn off by standing still. This day at the bank was already starting to pay off.

I wondered how Austin and Gus were doing with their research assignments today. There wasn't much time to plan everything. If we were going to pull off this robbery, it would have to be this Friday, the day of Brisbane's opening night party. So that meant we had a lot of quick studying to do.

I'd sent Austin to a place called "Flagler's Attack Dogs." I'd seen in Mom's notes that it was where the bank got its guard dogs. I wanted him to find out everything he could about rott-weilers, the breed of dog that protected the safe here at the bank.

Gus's job was to go to Groth and Lumstein, the architects who'd designed the inside of this bank. I told him to see what he could learn about the layout of the place. He was pretending to be a kid writing an essay on architecture. Hopefully, they'd be so proud of their design, that they'd want to show him every last detail of it. We had to know if there were any secret rooms or hidden hallways.

When Mom and I stepped out of the elevator, Mom met a man she knew. I remembered seeing him when I was with Mom trying to get the loan from Brisbane. He was the bank manager.

He seemed surprised to see Mom. "Molly," he said — that's Mom's name — "I didn't think you would come in today." I guess he figured she would be so angry with Brisbane that she'd never come back.

"Well, the party is Friday, and I need to get the system as close to operational as possible," she said.

The man stepped in closer to her and lowered

his voice. "I want you to know that I talked to Mr. Brisbane about the loan and he won't budge. I'm sorry."

"Thank you for asking," Mom said to him. She didn't look too surprised by this news. I think she already considered Brisbane a lost cause. This guy, the bank manager, seemed pretty nice, though. At least he'd tried to help her.

"Is this your daughter?" he asked.

"Yes, this is Maddy," Mom said.

"Hi. I'm Alan," he introduced himself. "How would you like a tour of the bank?"

"I'd love one," I said quickly. This was awesome! A tour of the bank was exactly what I needed. Mom was too busy to show me everything and Alan's offer of a tour was too good to be true. It was exactly what I needed.

Mom seemed hesitant. "I'm sure you're too busy," she said to him.

"That's okay. I'll take good care of her," he assured Mom with a smile.

"All right. Have fun," Mom said to me. "Thanks, Alan."

I went down the hall with Alan until we came to some doors that had security code panels next to them. I'd have to learn what these codes were before I could do anything. I supposed the simplest way to find out was to just ask him. "Who has the codes to all these doors?" I asked.

"They're different from room to room," he replied. Then he leaned down to me and whispered. "But I have a personal code that's good for the whole building."

He pressed in his code, and I made sure to watch what it was. He had typed in D-E-N-I-R-O.

Yes! I had the code for the whole building. That meant I had the security code for the safe! Awesome!

The door opened and we walked in. I recognized the office right away. It was Mr. Brisbane's office. I had been there just the other day when I went with Mom to ask him for the loan. "Isn't this Mr. Brisbane's office?" I asked.

"Yeah, but I like to sneak in here when I know he's in a meeting," Alan confessed. He went behind the desk and sat in Brisbane's huge chair, putting his hands behind his head like he owned the world.

"Look at the views," he added, pointing to the windows that overlooked the city. The entire city surrounded us. From here, we could see for miles.

I noticed a high-tech set of screens on the desk. They were like a mini version of the screens I'd seen back at the security desk. "Oh, and check this out," he said, moving the computer mouse on the desk. One by one, the screens lit up, showing different places in the bank. "Get this," he went on, "I can even control all the cameras from right here."

Yes! This was exactly the stuff I needed to know!

He clicked a button and his face came up on one of the screens. He had turned on the screen that monitored Brisbane's office. "Hi, there, Ferrell!" he waved to the camera.

We left Brisbane's office and went to Alan's office next. It was smaller, but I thought it was nicer. I noticed some framed photos on the wall and went closer to see what they were. One was a photo from the movie *Planet of the Apes*. "This is me," he said excitedly, pointing to the arm of an ape in the corner of the picture.

"Wow!" I cried, impressed. "You were in this movie?"

"I was the ape right next to that ape," he said.

He moved to the next photo, an ad that showed a mouth full of teeth. "That's my toothpaste ad."

"Those are your teeth?" I asked.

He smiled wide to show me that they were the same teeth. Then, his smile faded. "I don't know why I became a bank manager," he said. "My passion's always been acting. But things happen and . . . well, here I am."

"I think you'd make a really good actor," I said. He seemed sad about not acting anymore. "Oh, well," he said. "Let's get on with our tour."

We left his office and Alan led me down some marble stairs. We rounded a corner and went through a large, open safe door. As soon as we went through the door and into the bank tunnel, two rottweilers began barking like crazy. They were in a barred-off area, but they were scary just the same. Even Alan seemed afraid of them. "I can't wait until those dogs are gone," he said. "Once your mother has had a chance to fully test the security system, we can put Killer, Betsey, and Julio up for adoption."

"I only see one dog," I mentioned.

Alan looked and saw I was right. "Yeah," he said. "Julio might be in there." He pointed to another one of the bank tunnels. "That reminds me," he added. He took a cell phone from the inside pocket of his suit jacket and punched in some numbers. "Dodson, can you please tell Ferrell to lock up the dogs on Friday for the party. I don't want them ripping the throat out of one of the board members. Thank you."

That was excellent news. If he locked up the rottweilers it would be one less problem for us to deal with.

As we continued along, I tried to memorize every angle of the safe tunnels. I'd need to recall where everything was located if my plan was going to work. This was the old safe; it wasn't where the really big money was kept. That was the one I would have to find.

We continued walking, and after a while we wound up at my mother's empty office. "Okay, little lady," Alan said. "I guess someone's going to send out a search party if I don't get back to work. Can you wait here until your mom gets back?"

"Sure. Thank you," I said. In fact, I wanted to be here alone, waiting for her. Who knew what I could find out here in her office?

He smiled at me, waved, and walked off. He

was a really nice guy. I felt bad that he'd never gotten a chance to be an actor.

While I waited for Mom, I looked around. I discovered another video and played it on the TV in her office. I was in luck! It showed the tunnel leading into the new safe!

Just as it was about to show the safe room, Mom walked in. "You really are interested in security systems," she commented, turning off the video.

"Oh, not really," I disagreed. "I was just bored. I was actually hoping that was a rock video or something."

"Well, this shouldn't be out," she said as she tossed the video into her desk drawer and locked it. I'd been so close to seeing the safe!

For the rest of the day, I tried to learn everything I could about the bank. It wasn't easy since I was pretty much stuck in Mom's office.

At lunchtime, Mom and I passed the security desk on the way out and then, again, on the way in. I tried to hang around and talk to Chad to see what I could find out about the security system. All I really discovered was that I'd been right about his boss, Ferrell. He really was a bigger idiot than Chad. He thought he was some sort of super ninja of the security guard world. And he loved those vicious rottweilers.

When it was time to go, I was tired but super psyched about my plan. I had learned so much about the bank. But most important, I had learned the security code for the safe. I was in a very good mood.

"Did you have a good time with Alan Hartmann on the tour?" Mom asked while we drove home. She'd been so busy at the bank that we hadn't really talked until then.

"I know the code for the safe," I told her. I don't know why I said it. Maybe I couldn't resist bragging. I was so proud of myself for getting that code!

"Oh, yeah?" Mom challenged me. "What is it?"

"It's the name of that actor who was in *Meet the Parents* with Ben Stiller," I told her. I could picture him; he'd played the girl's father.

"Robert De Niro?" Mom asked.

"Yep, Deniro," I told her.

Mom grinned. "That doesn't get you into the safe, honey. I'm the only one with that code."

My good mood suddenly vanished.

Chapter 8

Austin

Maddy and I met in my room that night. I was completely exhausted from my day with the rottweilers. I'd pretended to be a kid interested in attack dogs, but I think the guy who owned the place was onto me. He practically let the dogs eat me alive. I ran out of there with vicious rottweilers nipping at my butt.

I did learn something that might be important, though. To get the dogs to stop attacking you have to say a really funny German word.

Aus-farht. It sounded like *ouch fart*, but it meant "to drive out." Hopefully, I wouldn't need to use it.

"Sorry, Austin," Maddy told me as she settled into a chair. "It turns out that the rottweilers will be locked up that night."

"Do you mean I got chased around by crazed dogs for nothing?" I cried.

"I don't know," she replied. "It's still better for us not to have to deal with the dogs."

"I guess," I said.

We waited for Gus. When he came in, he carried an actual scale model of the bank! "Score!" he boasted as he set it on my desk.

"Way to go!" Maddy cheered.

I was sort of annoyed. My day had been wasted because the rottweilers were now going to be tied up, and Gus had come out looking like the big winner.

The three of us sat on my bed, staring at the model. It was pretty great that he'd gotten it, although I'd never admit it to him. I came up with the idea of using superhero action figures to help us plan the robbery. Maddy had obviously given this plan lots of thought. She acted out the plan she'd devised, using the figures as us. It actually seemed like it might work.

Even though we'd gotten this far, I still couldn't believe we were really doing this. I guess Maddy must have been feeling the same way. "Do you think we can do it?" she asked suddenly. "Do you think we'll really get the money?"

Her words surprised me. Up until that second, she'd seemed superconfident. Suddenly, she was unsure. Maybe it was because it was getting so close.

I wanted to say "No way! We can't possibly do it!" But I looked into her big eyes, and she seemed so hopeful. How could I let her down? "Are you kidding? Of course!" I replied.

"Yeah, of course," Gus agreed, even though he sounded just as uncertain as I felt. Did he *always* have to say the same thing I said at the exact same moment that I said it? It was really getting on my nerves!

"We can't fail. I mean, come on, you're the best climber in the whole state," I said. "Who else could climb one hundred feet?"

"Yeah, and Austin is some freak-of-nature computer genius," Gus said. I didn't know whether to glare at him or thank him for calling me a genius.

I decided it was a compliment, and I tried to

return it. "Yeah and Gus is . . . Gus is . . . well . . ."

Just then Gus let out the biggest burp you ever heard. "Gus is disgusting," I finished. Gus pounded me on the arm, and I pounded him back.

"Get serious, guys," Maddy said. "Today, when I was in Brisbane's office with Alan, I realized how we could fool the security cameras into thinking Alan was in Brisbane's office. We're going to need a tape of him, and I have an idea how we can get it. Listen . . ."

The next day, the three of us rode our bikes to Alan Hartmann's house. We'd looked up his address in the phone book and had our fingers crossed that we'd found the right Alan Hartmann. We had some luck because the guy was out in his driveway washing his car when we walked our bikes up to his house.

"Yo! Mr. Hartmann!" Maddy called out to him. "Ready for your big break?"

I had my camcorder in its case and Gus had a big movie lamp with him. I took the camera from the case and waved it in the air to show him what Maddy had meant.

Mr. Hartmann smiled. He seemed like a good guy. "A great actor is always ready," he said. "Which one of you is the next Spielberg?" he asked.

"I am," I told him. "I'm shooting a movie for my film class and we need a talented adult to help with a role."

"Would you mind being in a scene for us?" Maddy asked.

"Sure."

It didn't take long to set up a backdrop in his garage. It was a hand-painted picture of Brisbane's office that Maddy had made that morning.

Gus rigged the lamp to the side of the garage. Hartmann had changed into a jacket, shirt, and tie, although he still had his shorts on. Maddy stood on the side, waiting to go on.

"Okay, this is the story," I said to Mr. Hartmann. "Maddy is playing a girl who is home alone and scared of the dark, so we've loaded the house with all sorts of burglar alarms. You play her dad who comes into her room just as the alarm blares. You're going to try to calm her down. So when I say 'Action,' you give us your line."

"What do I — I mean my character — what does he do for a living?" Alan Hartmann asked.

"I'm glad you asked," I said. Of course, I had no idea what his character did for a living. I was making all this up as I went along.

In the corner of the garage, I saw Gus roll his eyes. He didn't understand anything about creative people. I respected Mr. Hartmann for wanting to know about his character. "You work for a highly specialized branch of the CIA. You're an international spy — and a single father," I said.

Mr. Hartmann nodded thoughtfully. He was serious about getting his character just right. He was so sincere that I felt bad about tricking him like this, but it was for Maddy's father. That's what I kept reminding myself — that this was all for Mr. Philips.

"Do I have hair or no hair?" Mr. Hartmann asked as he lifted his toupee — from his head. It was freaky!

"Hair!" I said quickly. He put the wig piece back on, thank goodness. That was weird and funny. I had to try really hard not to laugh. I turned to Maddy just so I wouldn't have to look at Mr. Hartmann's wig for a moment. "As for your character, Maddy," I said, trying to keep a straight face, "she's been scared of the dark for years, ever since —"

"Austin, I know my character!" Maddy cried.

I think she just wanted to get this over with. But I was starting to get into it. Just like Gus, she obviously didn't have much patience with the creative process. "Very well," I said, a little coldly. "We're ready." I hit the RECORD button on my camera. "We have speed . . . and . . . action!"

We ran through the scene, and Mr. Hartmann was a real pro. It was too bad the guy was a bank manager because he was really good. We thanked him and headed home, walking our bikes away from his house.

Everything had gone so well, and Maddy was in a great mood. Seeing her so happy made me feel awesome. "You're good, Austin," she said. "You were really good!"

Once again, Gus rolled his eyes. *He* certainly didn't understand a thing about the artistic process. But who cared — as long as Maddy appreciated my talent? She turned to me and did something that stopped me in my tracks.

She kissed me!

Okay, it was a kiss on the cheek — but just the same. I froze, amazed.

I guess the kiss surprised Gus, too. He dropped the movie lamp and stared at us. Then he stomped away, wheeling his bike off with him.

"Gus! Where are you going?" Maddy called after him. He didn't answer; he didn't even look back. I was glad to see him go. Now that Maddy had finally revealed how she felt about me, I didn't see how Gus and I could go on working together. It would just be too difficult for him.

"Come back," she called after him. "We need to talk about the rest of the plan."

He whirled around angrily to face her. "Talk about the rest of the plan with your *boyfriend* there," he snapped.

"What?" Maddy shouted. "He's not my boyfriend!"

Not her boyfriend? What about the kiss? And the way she said it was horrible — as if the thought of my being her boyfriend was ridiculous.

A second ago I'd been the happiest guy in the world. Now I felt like sinking into a hole and letting the dirt cover me up. "So you'd rather go out with Gus!?" I shouted.

Maddy looked at both of us with a disgusted expression on her face. "Are all boys this stupid?" she yelled. "I don't want to go out with *either* of you!"

I stepped next to Gus. Normally, I'd never — ever — think of Gus and me as being on the same side. But suddenly it seemed we were. Maddy, the girl we both worshiped, had just rejected both of us. She'd broken our hearts — both of them at the same time!

"If we're so stupid, why don't you rob the bank on your own?" Gus said angrily.

"Good one," I said to him. "You tell her."

Maddy folded her arms. "Fine! I will!"

"Yeah? Good luck rigging your go-cart," Gus shouted.

"And I hope you have a good time hacking into the mainframe of the bank's computer by yourself," I added, getting into the spirit of things.

Gus turned to me. "This is the dumbest bank robbery ever. Come on, Austin."

Together we walked our bikes away from Maddy. It was weird, but true. I was walking away from Maddy Philips, the girl I'd adored since forever, and leaving with . . . Gus!

We walked on together without talking until we couldn't see Maddy anymore.

Every once in a while, Gus and I looked at each other, but we had nothing to say. After all, we were only together because we were both mad at Maddy. And we were both mad at Maddy because each of us wanted to be her boyfriend.

After a while, we came to the go-cart track. As we approached it, I noticed the front was still gated closed and about ten kids had gathered outside on the sidewalk. Gus and I looked at each other. What was going on?

"What's happening?" Gus asked the kids as we joined them.

Before anyone could answer him, a man slapped a big padlock on the front gate. "Hey! What do you think you're doing?" Gus shouted at the man.

He slowly turned and looked at us. "The owners couldn't keep up the payments," he said. "The bank's closing." He stuck a sign up on the gate. It said "Closed."

Suddenly, I felt pretty rotten for abandoning Maddy and her family. I had the feeling Gus was feeling the same way.

Chapter 9

Maddy

What a rotten day it had been. Austin and Gus had deserted me. I couldn't believe they would just walk off like that. Boys!

All my life I'd thought of them as my two best friends. I never thought of them like *that*. To be completely honest, lately I'd started to suspect that they both kind of liked me — *liked* me — but I just kind of ignored it. I never thought it was that big a deal to them.

One thing was for sure, though. They had been right when they said I couldn't pull off the bank robbery without them. There was just no way. Now I didn't know how I would get the money for Dad's operation.

Mom had dropped me off at the hospital to stay with Dad while she picked up a few things at the grocery store. He'd fallen asleep, so I got up to get myself a drink of water from the bathroom.

While I was in there filling up a cup, a nurse and Dad's doctor moved near the room. I could hear them talking, even though they didn't see me. "What should we do now?" the nurse asked the doctor.

"He's slipping faster than we thought," the doctor replied. "If the family doesn't get him into that clinic by the weekend . . . well, the best we can do is make him comfortable."

I staggered back, leaning against the sink. I had to get that money, and I'd have to do whatever it took. There was no way I'd let Dad die because of something as stupid as money.

When I stepped out of the bathroom, the doctor and nurse had gone. I looked at Dad, who was still asleep.

"Dad, I want to talk to you," I said softly, sitting on the bed beside him. I knew he didn't hear me, but I needed to talk to him so badly. "I'm going to steal a quarter of a million bucks from Mom's bank. I'm going to have to climb one hundred feet — higher than I've ever climbed — to get to the safe. And I'm going to have to lie to my two best friends to get them to do it with me."

My voice shook a little when I said that last thing. I felt guilty about it, but I *was* going to lie to them. I'd made up my mind the moment I'd heard the doctor and the nurse talking.

I was going to tell both Austin and Gus what they both wanted to hear so that they'd help me. I planned to tell each one that I was in love with him. I felt terrible about it, but I was doing it for Dad. Austin and Gus would both survive if I lied to them. But Dad wouldn't survive if I *didn't* lie.

I wondered what Dad would say to me if he had heard me. I said out loud what I thought he might reply. I lowered my voice and spoke in his voice. "Well, Maddy, a hundred feet is too dangerous. That's how far I fell. Lying to your two best friends isn't good, either. Plus, it's illegal to steal. And Mom will get fired if anyone finds out what you've done."

I knew everything he would have said was true. What I was doing was terribly wrong. But if he could get better, wouldn't it all be worth it? Somehow I'd find a way to make it up to everyone. Right now, though, Dad was all that mattered. I kissed his forehead, sure of what I needed to do.

The next day, I went to Austin's house. He was in his backyard filming a squirrel that was leaping from branch to branch.

He definitely saw me come into the yard, but he just kept filming. I guess he was still pretty angry.

I gently pushed his camera down so he couldn't ignore me any longer. "I need to talk to you," I said.

He picked his camera up again and went back to filming. I got the message — loud and clear. But it didn't matter because I was going to make him listen to me no matter what it took.

"Austin," I began, "I've been thinking since yesterday and . . ." I took a deep breath. "I've decided I'm in love with you."

Austin put down his camera and stared at me, wide-eyed. I hated lying to him, but he wouldn't help me otherwise, and I was desperate.

"But . . . but, what about Gus?" he asked.

"He's cute, sure, but you're the smart one," I told him. That was true. Gus *was* cute and Austin *was* smart.

I took half a friendship heart on a chain from my pocket and handed it to him. "Wear this around your neck," I said, placing it over his head. "This means that we're a couple. I have the other half."

Austin lifted his camera and aimed it at me. "Please say all that again," he requested.

I didn't want my lie caught on film, so I pushed the camera away and kissed him lightly. "Promise to help me with my mission?" I asked.

Austin nodded.

"Good. Don't say anything to Gus, though. He's still in love with me, and we need him. And don't show him the heart," I warned him.

"I won't," Austin replied.

I left him there and headed for Gus's house, next to mine. I saw him in his yard and spoke to him over the fence that separates our houses. Just like with Austin, I told him that I realized I was in love with him.

"But what about Austin?" Gus asked.

"Sure, he's smart," I said. "But I've been in love with you the whole time."

Gus's face lit up with a smile. "I knew it! Yes!" he cried.

I felt so low for lying to him like this. If it wasn't a matter of life and death, I never would have done it. I took out the other half of the friendship heart that I'd given to Austin and I handed it over the fence to Gus. "Here. I have the other half." I went up on my toes and kissed him lightly. "Promise to help me with the mission?" I asked.

Gus nodded. He was definitely back in.

"Don't tell Austin," I said, "or show him the heart, okay. He's not going to help if he finds out about us."

"I won't say a word," Gus promised.

Chapter 10

Gus

Now that I knew Maddy loved me, there wasn't anything I wouldn't do for her. We headed down to the go-cart track and used Maddy's keys to get in by the side door, the door they'd forgotten to padlock.

I worked like crazy all day to get the go-carts tuned up and ready for the big bank robbery. It was cool working on the go-carts with Maddy helping me. They were going to be what you might call our "getaway cars."

We phoned Austin, and he joined us there at

about four o'clock. I had fixed up a go-cart for him, one for Maddy, and one for myself.

The first thing I had to do was teach Austin and Maddy how to drive a go-cart. "Watch me," I told them. I drove around the track at top speed. I guess you could say I was showing off for Maddy. I pulled up to Austin and Maddy and pushed back my helmet. "Now it's your turn, Austin," I said.

Austin got into his go-cart and stepped on the accelerator. Oh, man! He was zooming all over the track and screaming in fear.

"I definitely have a lot of work ahead of me," I told Maddy.

Maddy nodded, looking worried, as Austin continued speeding around in all directions.

Maddy was a natural in the go-cart. She'd driven one before and just needed to practice. It was good that she didn't need help because I had to work with Austin for three more hours before he got the hang of driving the go-cart.

The sun was setting by the time we left the track. The three of us walked along the river toward Austin's house, talking about our plans.

"Before I came to the track I spent hours on my computer. I managed to get all the information we needed and downloaded it onto my cell phone," Austin said.

Austin is a true genius, I have to give him that. He was trying to impress Maddy with his braininess. Now that I knew Maddy's true feelings, I felt sorry for him. It was kind of pathetic, really.

"Are you sure you're going to be able to control the cameras?" Maddy asked him.

"Absolutely," he replied.

"Good," Maddy said. "Now all I need is Mom's code. How do people choose a code?"

I thought hard, trying to remember anything I'd ever heard about codes. Even though Maddy was in love with me, she still thought of Austin as the smart one. I wanted her to be impressed by my brains, too. Unfortunately, my brain wasn't coming up with any answers about codes.

"People pick the things that are important to them," Austin said, as if he were some kind of authority on the subject of codes.

"I wonder what's most important to Mom," Maddy said. "What would be important enough for her to use as a code word?"

"It's the small, personal things that mean the most to the modern woman," Austin went on, still trying to sound like he knew what he was talking about.

Brainiac might have thought he was impressing Maddy, but that was the dumbest thing I'd ever heard, and I told him so. Maddy rolled her eyes. She must have thought it was pretty goofy, too.

"It's just something I read somewhere," Austin said sulkily. I was glad he'd stopped acting like the world's biggest authority on codes.

The more I thought about it, though, the more I thought Austin might be onto something. People *did* pick codes based on the things that were important to them. "Ask her about her favorite pet," I suggested.

"I already thought of that," Maddy said. "Last night she told me that she had a hamster named Harriet and a hedgehog named Sean and an imaginary friend named Wolfgang."

"Wolfgang?" I asked.

Maddy shrugged. "What can I say? Mom is weird."

"Do you think any of those names are her code?" I asked.

"I don't know," she admitted. "Maybe."

"No," Austin disagreed. "Her code is probably

something more important to her than a hamster or hedgehog."

"I guess," Maddy said. "Maybe it's Max."

We kept walking but not talking. It seemed to me that all three of us were thinking hard about our part of the plan. I know *I* was.

Maddy wanted me to rig up a miniature go-cart that could be driven by remote control. That way the motion of the car would turn on the cameras all over the bank. It seemed to me that there had to be a way to connect the go-cart controls to a Playstation controller to make it move as fast and as smooth as a go-cart in a video game.

We arrived at Austin's house and went to his room. He had rigged an old-fashioned red, yellow, and green TV projector to a hook on his ceiling. I wasn't really sure what he was going to do with it.

"Let's hope this works," he said as he shut off the lights and turned on the projector. An open, 3-D model of the bank was projected into midair over our heads. Austin used his computer mouse to rotate the model.

"Whoa! Awesome!" I cried. Then I noticed that Maddy's jaw had dropped open and she looked up at the model in amazement. I didn't want her to be *that* impressed. "I mean, it's all right," I said more coolly.

Maddy went to the model and pointed to a large room. "Here's where the party is going to be. We have to get past Chad to get to the ninth floor where the safe is."

I made a disgusted face. It was the face I always made when someone mentioned Chad.

Maddy walked around the model until she came to Brisbane's office. She pointed to it. "Austin, you have to get here, to Brisbane's office, to operate the cameras while Gus and I head for the safe."

Austin shot me a nasty look. He'd obviously noticed that Maddy wanted *me* to go with her to the safe while *he* stayed behind. It made sense that she'd want to be with the guy she dug, but, like I said, I had to feel a little sorry for the guy.

"I've got to go now," Maddy said suddenly.

"Why?" I asked. I was looking forward to walking home with her from Austin's house.

"I'll meet you tomorrow at the track, but tonight I want to practice climbing the water tower," she said. "When I climb to the safe, it's going to be higher than I've ever climbed. I need to practice."

Chapter 11

Maddy

That night, I nearly made it to the top of the water tower. Nearly. I had only fifteen feet more to go to get to the top. I was determined to make it, but I just couldn't. My muscles ached, and I felt completely worn out.

Resting my forehead against the cool metal tank of the tower, I sighed. Mom had said that safe was one hundred feet up, that was almost twice as high as this tower. How would I climb that far if I couldn't even scale this tower?

I came down again, and it was slow going. I

felt like my muscles were going to cramp up —
and that would have been a disaster. It would
be a total and complete disaster if it happened
tomorrow in the bank. I wished I'd had a chance
to see that safe. I couldn't imagine how it could
be that high up. I wondered how Mom had come
up with an idea like that. Maybe it had occurred
to her because Dad and I love to climb.

It was getting late so I tried sneaking into the
house.

But when I came to the doorway, Mom was
sitting in the living room with my climbing harness on her lap — and boy was she furious.

I don't know how she'd found it behind the
shed, but somehow she had. "Have you been lying to me all this time?" she demanded.

"Mom . . . I . . ." I had no idea what to say.

"Look what happened to your dad!" Mom
shouted as she stood and let the harness fall to
the floor. "And now you're doing the same thing!
I know you, Maddy —"

"You don't know anything about me!" I yelled
back at her. I don't know why I shouted at her like
that. "I'll bet you go months without even thinking about me!" I accused her. "You only care about
two things — your stupid job and the baby!"

Whoa! I hadn't wanted to say those things.

The stunned look on Mom's face told me that I'd really gotten to her. I felt so guilty and so confused that I didn't know what to do, so I ran to my bedroom and slammed the door behind me. I threw myself onto my bed and before I even hit the mattress, I was asleep.

The next morning I woke up and walked into the living room. Mom was already up and sitting at the table. I wondered if she was mad at me. She looked tense.

"They're going to do a lot of tests on Dad at the hospital tonight, and I want to be there for that. You're going to have to watch Max after day care while I'm gone," she said with a worried look on her face. My jaw dropped. This was going to totally mess up the plan!

"I . . . I can't. I'm going out with Gus and Austin. We're . . . going to the movies."

"If you're going to the movies, you're going to have to watch something Max can see, too," said Mom.

"But . . . I can't! I'm going to —" I stammered, but Mom cut me off.

"Maddy, you're going to baby-sit Max tonight after you pick him up from day care and that's that!" Mom said, staring at me as if to say "End of story!" She picked up her briefcase and began to walk out the door. I just stood there, calculating, pondering how to make the plan work around this problem. Mom put her hand on the doorknob, then paused and turned around, looking at me.

"One other thing," she said. I tensed up, and my breath caught in my throat. What else could possibly go wrong?

"I do think about you, Maddy. Everyday. All the time." She looked at me a moment, then walked out the door, shutting it lightly behind her. I let my breath out with a gush of air. That was nice and all, but I had other things to deal with at the moment.

That evening, I got Max from day care and went down to the track with him. I'd given Gus and Austin my keys, so they were already there when Max and I arrived. I noticed that Gus had tied a bandana around his neck to hide the half heart chain that I'd given him.

"What's he . . ." Austin asked as he stared at Max and then at to me.

"I have to baby-sit."

"But . . ."

"Save it. He'll be fine. He's never made a sound in his life. I've got his bottle, and he'll be happy as long as he has it," I said, holding out the spare bottle as if it were solid proof of Max's ability to be quiet.

"What if he messes up?" Austin asked.

"We're my dad's only chance," I said firmly. I gave him my "we're doing this whether you like it or not" look.

Gus stopped tinkering with the go-cart and stood up. He looked like a very young repairman in a goofy bandanna. "Okay, I'm ready," he stated as he wiped his hands on his jeans.

"Ready," Austin said quietly, standing up next to Gus.

I faced them both, shifting Max so he rested on my hip. "Let's hit it," I said.

Chapter 12

Austin

We zoomed down the street, Maddy in the lead, Gus and I following. Max sat in Maddy's lap in a miniature helmet just his size. We reached the bank and whizzed around the corner into the parking garage in the back, dodging the traffic of limos and fancy cars that had arrived for the party. There were lots of people, women in expensive-looking dresses and men in tuxedos with black ties.

We quickly reached the parking garage gate. This was the first step of the plan — to get in without getting caught. I took a deep breath and pressed the gas pedal.

The carts are too loud, I thought. *We were going to get caught for sure.* Thankfully, though, the security guard was watching some sitcom at his little desk, and he laughed along with the laugh track from the show.

I pressed the gas pedal, urging the cart to go faster and faster. I checked to make sure the guard hadn't followed us and sighed with relief when I didn't see him. My sigh was cut short as we shot under the orange-and-white–striped guard arm, barely making it. We veered sharply to the left, leaving skid marks on the pavement as we turned onto the spiral ramp. I looked back again and caught a glimpse of a very confused-looking guard, but we were out of there before he got a chance to notice. The first step of the plan was complete.

As we raced down the ramp, I couldn't help but grin proudly at my camera and the mount I'd rigged for it on my go-cart. I was filming all this high-speed action. My eyes flicked to the flip screen. I had a perfect shot of us whizzing down the ramp.

Before long, we were out of our go-carts and

getting ready to enter the party. We'd bought the cheapest fancy clothing we could find at the local thrift store. Our looks weren't quite perfect, but close enough. Maddy was dressed in a red, formal dress, which in my opinion, made her look even more awesome then she normally did. Gus and I both wore a dinner jacket and dress pants. Frankly, I thought I looked better than he did. Max gurgled and poked at the little black satin tie we had given him to go along with a mini tuxedo we'd found.

Maddy took a deep breath and looked at us. I offered my arm like a gentleman. Gus picked up Max with one arm and took Maddy's arm with the other. All linked up, we walked to the bank entrance.

At the front door, we ducked behind some bushes to see if the coast was clear. Some puffy, important-looking people were jabbering away to the guards, who laughed heartily. This was our chance to get in while the guards were distracted. We came out from behind the bushes and hurried through the doorway before the guards could notice us.

Step two of the plan was complete.

Inside, the elegant guests stayed on the left,

in the finished part of the bank. We walked casually over to the massive black curtain to the right and ducked behind it quickly. No one noticed.

Behind the curtain were plastic sheets and scaffolds. Max sneezed, and dust flew all around him. Maddy started to climb a nearby scaffold as Gus, Max, and I watched her from down below. I did a quick scan of the area to make sure there were no cameras that could mess up our plan. Suddenly, a red light caught my eye. It was a security camera, and it had picked up on our motion!

"Maddy!" I whispered, my voice panic-stricken. Maddy looked down. Her eyes widened to the size of saucers when she saw the camera.

"Don't move!" she whispered urgently. She started climbing fast. She was already out of the camera's range, but we weren't. I didn't move a muscle — I didn't even blink.

We knew that Chad and his boss, Ferrell, were going to be on duty at the security desk on the mezzanine that night. We'd thought of a way to get rid of one guard, and now was the time to do it.

In just a few more minutes, Maddy had

reached the mezzanine and climbed over the side into a little waiting area. My walkie-talkie crackled to life. "Come in, Maddy," I whispered.

"Austin, I need to get Ferrell away from the security desk," Maddy said to me over the walkie-talkie.

I looked up, and I could see that Ferrell was showing Chad some kind of martial arts moves. That guy thought he was a real ninja. Then I remembered the remote-control car we'd brought along. It might be just the thing we needed.

"Gus, give me the car," I said, putting Max down on the floor. He pulled it out of the bag. But how would we get it to Maddy? "Give me your sock," I said to him.

He undid his sneaker and pulled off his sock. I held my nose. "The way your feet smell," I said, "it's not normal." I stuffed the remote and the controller into the sock. "Toss this up to Maddy," I told Gus. He's got a better arm than I do.

Gus threw the little car with one swing. "The car is on the mezzanine," I spoke into the walkie-talkie.

"Roger that," Maddy responded. "Ew! This sock stinks! I'm about to drive the remote-control car down the steps."

The idea was that the car would set off the motion-detecting monitors. That would distract the guards so that Gus and I could run up the stairs to the elevator.

Maddy was close to the security desk. I couldn't see her because she was crouched down low, but she had left her walkie-talkie channel open and I could hear Chad and Ferrell talking.

"The car is going," Maddy reported.

The plan was working! The monitors at the security desk were quickly coming on. "What's going on?" I heard Ferrell ask. "Why are those monitors going on?"

"I don't see anything," Chad said.

"That's when your enemies are the most dangerous, when you can't see them," Ferrell said.

As he stood, I could see his electric baton. That thing looked scary. Ferrell seemed very fond of it.

"This is a test, I just know it," he went on. "I'll go downstairs and make a round. You stay here." He left the desk and headed down the hall. "It's hunt or be hunted," he shouted back to Chad.

"It worked. Chad's alone at the guard station," Maddy reported over the walkie-talkie.

"Be ready and wait until I give you a sign," she added.

"Sign?" I didn't remember anything in our plan about a sign. "What sign?" I asked into the walkie-talkie.

Before she could reply, Gus grabbed the walkie-talkie from me. "Maddy, stay away from Chad. He's a lunatic!"

But Maddy didn't answer. She'd already turned off the walkie-talkie. We could see her walking toward Chad.

I turned to Gus. "What sign?" I asked. He shook his head and shrugged.

Chapter 13

Maddy

I walked quietly up to the security desk where Gus's brother Chad sat by himself. His boss, Ferrell, had gone off to see what was setting off all the security screens. Of course, he didn't know it was the small remote-control car that I'd sent zooming through the bank. "Hi," I said when I was right behind him.

I guess I'd startled Chad because he jumped, knocking things off the desk. "What are you doing here?"

"I was at the party and I was totally bored," I said with a smile. "What are you doing?"

"Just my job," he replied stiffly.

I casually leaned against the desk. "Why do you have to be such a jerk to your brother?"

Chad grinned at me as if he were proud of the way he treated Gus.

"You know he completely idolizes you," I said. I guess you could say I was trying to butter him up. I'd never really heard Gus say one nice thing about Chad. "To him you're like Kobe or Shaq. But you're too busy making fun of him to see it."

"You're lying. He thinks I'm an idiot," Chad said.

He had that right, but I couldn't let him know it. "Nope, you're his hero," I continued. "You're his hero, and he thinks you're going to make a great cop. He told me, and I agree with him."

A big smile came across Chad's face. He was buying it.

"You should come downstairs with me," I suggested. "The police chief is here to check out Mom's security system. You could show him how serious you are about your job."

He got up from behind the desk, and we began walking down the stairs toward the party. At the bottom of the stairs, I spotted Gus, Max, and Austin hiding behind a column. I gave them the signal — a wink. For a second, I was afraid that they'd forgotten the signal because they didn't move. But then, when Chad and I had passed them, they ran up the stairs to the elevator.

Down at the party, I pointed Chad toward the police chief. Once I'd sent him on his way, I turned and raced up the stairs, taking them three at a time. Austin held the elevator door open for me as I jumped in. All right! Onto the next phase of our mission.

In the elevator, we peeled off our formal wear and got down to the all-black thief outfits we wore underneath. Even Max was all in black. We couldn't be too careful.

The doors opened on the ninth floor, and we headed down the hallway. As we went, we secured our earpieces so we could communicate with one another. When we got to Brisbane's office, I punched in the code Alan had showed me. D–E–N–I–R–O.

It worked! We were in! Austin got to work plugging his video camera into Brisbane's computer. Gus tested the battery on his drill, and I settled Max onto Brisbane's big, swiveling chair.

"I'll be back," I told him. "I just need to bust this bank so we can save Dad." Max dropped his bottle and, for a moment, I was nervous that he was going to fuss. I gave it back to him, and he smiled.

"Okay, Austin," I said. "Gus and I are on our way." He shot us a thumbs-up sign as we went out into the hall again. I led the way down to the staircase Alan had showed me. It was the one that went to the old safe door. We crept low to the wall so the cameras wouldn't see us.

"Austin?" I spoke into my headset.

"Check," he replied.

"Do you see any dogs in the room ahead of us?" I knew Ferrell was supposed to have locked them up tonight, but I didn't want any nasty surprises.

"It's clear," he reported. "Go!"

We saw the security camera swivel up to the ceiling. Austin was controlling it from Brisbane's office. Suddenly the camera swerved downward so it was pointed right at us. "What the heck!" Gus cried as we jumped back, out of the way.

"Sorry," Austin's voice came into my headset. "Max hit the mouse with his bottle."

The camera turned back to the ceiling, and Gus and I scrambled down the hall. When we got to the end, we found a door with a control panel — but there were no numbers on the control panel. Uh-oh.

And to make things even worse, Brisbane and Ferrell were coming down the hall — with three rottweilers! Gus and I looked at each other with panicked expressions. "Come on," I whispered sharply. I headed for a supply closet I'd noticed the other day. We climbed inside.

"What are these creatures doing out of their room?" Brisbane asked Ferrell.

"There was a disturbance, so I took them out to investigate with me," Ferrell explained.

"Well, take them downstairs where they belong," Brisbane said irritably.

"But, sir . . . ," Ferrell started to object. He was really into those dogs.

"Do you want to be out on the street?" Brisbane snapped at him. "No? Then do as I say."

Ferrell walked off with the dogs, muttering angrily. Brisbane left, too.

We stuck our heads out of the closet. Austin's voice came into my headset. "All clear," he said. "They're gone."

We went back to the door. "Now what?" Gus asked.

"I don't know," I admitted. How could we get into a room with no controls? Knowing the access code wouldn't even get us into this.

I didn't know what to do next. But I couldn't believe this was the end of the plan. There *had* to be a way in. I waved my hand over the control panel because I couldn't think of anything else to do.

The panel began to glow. Yes! I was onto something!

"Wow! Cool!" Gus cried. The keypad projected as a hologram in midair. The letters suddenly floated right in front of us. "Are you sure there aren't any dogs waiting for us on the other side of the door?" Gus asked.

"I guess we're going to find out," I replied.

Gus swallowed hard. He typed D–E–N–I–R–O onto the floating, holographic keys. The door in front of us slid open, and we stepped into the huge rooms. Gus and I checked in all directions. So far, there were still no dogs.

The place was really big, and high, and awesome. Safety deposit boxes lined the walls. "Where's the money?" Gus asked.

I didn't know. But Mom had said it was 100 feet up, so I gazed upward, and there it was! The safe hung in the air, suspended from the ceiling by four girders.

"Brilliant, Mom," I said, impressed. It would be the ultimate climb!

Chapter 14

Gus

That safe was crazy high. "It's too high, Maddy," I said. "There's got to be a way to bring it down."

She dropped to her knees and began searching the ground. I figured she was looking for a switch or something that would lower the safe. "Help me," she said. I walked toward her, but then stopped. It was ridiculous. We'd never find it.

I looked down and saw that I was standing on a mosaic of a lion. *I get it*! I thought. This was the Lyons Bank and the lion was their symbol. I took another step and suddenly the lion's eyes, began to glow.

Then something really wild happened. Glass panels rose up out of the floor and encircled Maddy and me. Glowing numbers covered the panels.

"I bet these numbers are to the safety-deposit boxes," Maddy said as she reached up to touch one of them. She hit a number and it began changing color. Over on the wall, a safety-deposit box slid forward. She was right!

Maddy walked out of the circle of glass panels and went to the safety-deposit box that had just come toward us. She studied the wall a minute, then turned toward me. "Hit twenty-three fifty-seven," she said.

It took a sec, but I found it. When I touched the number, it began to change color. Another safety-deposit box came forward. I suddenly re-alized what Maddy was thinking. The box she'd asked for was to the right of the first box, but just a little higher — it looked like a stair.

Maddy was one smart girl! I looked at her and grinned, and she smiled back at me.

She called numbers out and I touched them

on the panels. Before long she had a staircase of boxes leading halfway up to the safe. She still had to climb it, though. She'd have to scale the wall with just the boxes to balance on.

Maddy had had a great idea, but it still looked pretty dangerous to me. She seemed to know what I was thinking. "I'm climbing it," she said in that stubborn way she has. I knew there was nothing I could say that would stop her unless I found another way to get the safe down.

"Austin," I spoke into my headset, "you've got to tap into the main-whatever and find a way to bring the safe down. Maddy's going to kill herself."

"I'll work on it, but I don't really know how," Austin answered.

By the time I'd finished talking to Austin, Maddy was already in her climbing harness. She got up the first half of the boxes pretty quickly, and then started calling out numbers to me. As they slid forward, she climbed higher and higher.

It was amazing how that girl could climb. She was really brave. I was more into her than ever.

Finally, she reached the top of the wall. Maddy pulled out her winged climbing locks and prepared to cross the ceiling to the safe. But as she leaned forward, a blaring alarm sounded.

We looked at each other with panicked expressions.

"Austin, play the tape!" I shouted over my walkie-talkie.

Chapter 15

Austin

This was bad. I heard Gus but I couldn't play the tape. That was because I wasn't at the desk. I was hiding *under* the desk with Max in my lap.

Alan Hartmann had come in with his date from the party. Luckily, I'd been able to hide before he saw Max and me. Gus told me to play the tape again, but his voice was so loud, I was afraid Hartmann would hear him talking. I hoped neither of them would want to sit at the desk.

"So this is Mr. Brisbane's office?" Hartmann said, as he walked his date into the office. He stood right next to the desk. I could have reached out and tapped him on the leg.

I was dying there under the desk. Maddy and Gus needed me, but I couldn't do anything to help them.

"I finally have you to myself," Hartmann's date said.

"Mama!" Max said. I covered Max's mouth as quickly as I could. I thought he was the kid who couldn't talk. It figured he'd pick this second to start making noise.

Then there was a knock on the door! I closed my eyes. If it was Ferrell with the dogs, they'd sniff us out in a second. My heart was beating so loud, I wouldn't have been surprised if Hartmann could hear it.

But it was a woman. "Mr. Brisbane, are you . . . oh, Mr. Hartmann."

"Hello . . . I, uh," Hartmann stammered. He'd been caught using Brisbane's office. "Well, that completes our tour of the ninth floor," he told the woman as he and his date hurried out of the office.

I took a deep breath and put Max back up on

the chair. They couldn't hear the alarm in the rest of the bank, but I knew the security guards heard it.

I had to find a way to shut it off. The tape. Where was the tape?

I turned on my walkie-talkie. "Guys, what's going on?" I asked.

"Put on the tape!" Gus shouted over the set.

Chapter 16

Gus

Austin's voice came over my headset. "Here it is! It fell on the floor." I didn't hear him for a moment, but then he came back on. "I've got it under control. The tape is rolling!" he reported.

My shoulders sagged with relief. I couldn't believe he'd taken so long. "What was the problem?" I asked.

"Forget it," he said. "It's over."

The plan was to roll the tape of Mr. Hartmann in Brisbane's office. It was the one we'd filmed in Mr. Hartmann's garage. Austin had rigged it up when he tapped into Brisbane's computer. We'd had Mr. Hartmann say, "Take it easy. It's only me. Shut the alarms."

In another minute, the alarm shut off. It worked! I let out a long sigh of relief and glanced up at Maddy. She nodded at me and began to move across the wall above the safe.

It was so high that it made me dizzy just to look up at her. She was about ten feet above the safe and was going to have to drop down onto it. But before she could do that, she had to move hand over hand across the girders that held it.

I watched her go, shining a flashlight in the dark to help her see. At one point, she stopped and seemed to freeze in panic. But then she continued until she was hanging over the safe.

That was when her hand slipped.

I cried out as she fell through the air.

"Gus!" Austin shouted over the headset. He'd heard me yell.

Maddy fell onto the edge of the safe with a thud. She stayed there a moment, but she couldn't hold on because there was nothing to grip. She slid over the side onto the safe's front, grabbed on to the lock, and clung to it. My heart was crashing into my chest. I couldn't imagine what Maddy must feel like.

"She's okay," I reported to him.

Austin's voice came over the headset again. "Oh, no!" he cried. "She's triggered a timer. Gus! She has thirty seconds to enter a code or the alarm goes off!"

"You've got to reach the keypad in thirty seconds, or you'll set off an alarm," I told her.

Maddy hung on to the safe with one hand as she pointed out into the air. At first I couldn't figure out what she was doing. Then I saw it — another holographic keypad!

The letters floated in the air. These were the letters Maddy had to reach in less than 30 seconds!

Chapter 17

Maddy

As long as I didn't look down, I'd be okay. At least, that's what I kept telling myself as I clung to the bottom of the safe by one hand.

I reached out, straining to touch the holographic keypad. I was able to pull myself up just enough to reach the floating letters. But there was still a pretty major problem I was facing. . . .

I had no idea what the code was for the safe.

What would Mom pick as a code? I tried typing in M-A-X-W-E-L-L. Nothing. I tried H-A-R-R-I-E-T Harriet, her hamster. No.

Time was running out, and I couldn't hold on much longer. "Come on, Maddy, think!" I muttered. I typed in T-O-M. That's my dad's name, but that wasn't it, either.

I had one last idea. I didn't think it would work, but I couldn't think of anything else, and I was just about out of time. I touched the keys and typed in M-A-D-E-L-I-N-E.

The safe door began to slide open!

My name! Mom had used *my* name as the code for the most important job she'd ever had in her life!

I swung up, hooking my leg onto the safe and pulling myself in. A light had come on inside the safe. There was more money in that safe than I'd ever seen — ever even imagined — in my life! I pulled a nylon bag from my belt and set it on the floor of the safe.

My hands shook as I began counting out the amount I wanted — $250,000 dollars — just enough for Dad's operation. I mean, I could have taken millions, but I only wanted what I needed.

In minutes, I'd stuffed about $100,000 into a

bag and then dropped it down to Gus. I crossed my fingers, hoping the bag wouldn't break open when it hit the ground. It was so heavy and it was such a long way down. But it held together.

I opened a second nylon bag and filled it. I couldn't believe this was really happening. I actually had my hands on the money Dad needed. It was like an awesome dream come true.

Once I'd dropped the second bag to Gus, I anchored a rope to one of the girders and slid down. We each picked up a heavy bag of money and headed for the door. "On the move," Gus said to Austin on the walkie-talkie.

We were halfway down the hall when an alarm started to blare. Both of us froze. Red security lights came on all around us.

The door to the safe, the one we just left, slid closed. Then the door at the other end of the tunnel began closing. In a second, we'd be trapped.

We raced to the closing door and dove under it just as it closed. It was a close call!

All of a sudden, the door ahead of us swung open. Gus and I tensed, expecting security guards. But it was Austin with Max in his arms. "Mama! Mama!" Max called out, laughing.

"He hasn't said one word in his life, and now he won't shut up," Austin complained as he joined us. "You set off an exit alarm."

I took Max from him. "Let's go see Dad," I said to my little brother. Suddenly, I heard a vicious growl come from behind us. All four of us turned at once and saw three enormous rottweilers.

They lined up side by side, blocking the only way out. Behind us were the aisles of the old safety deposit boxes. I know it's insane to try to outrun a dog, but I couldn't think of anything else to do. "Run!" I yelled, clutching Max in my arms. The three of us ran like we'd never run in our lives, racing up and down the aisles.

The dogs chased right behind us. It didn't take long for them to box us into a corner. There was nothing left but to huddle there and wait for the dogs to get us.

"Aus-farht!" Austin yelled in a perfect-sounding German accent.

It worked. The dogs stopped. I looked at Austin, impressed. That was the halt command he'd learned from the attack-dog place.

But Ferrell walked in behind the dogs and, once again, we were trapped. On his face was a pleased sneer. "What do we have here?" he said.

"It's not what you think," I told him. "We were at the party."

"Save it, doll face," he said. Chad came in and stood beside his boss. "Well, Chad," Ferrell said. "It looks like we've caught our first little trespassers." His lips curled into a mean smile. "Now, what we're going to do is —"

He reached to his belt for his electric baton, but it wasn't there. Chad had quietly taken it from him and now held it in his hands. "Missing something, Ferrell?" he asked.

Ferrell's eyes widened with surprise as Chad zapped him. He fell to the floor like a sack of potatoes.

We looked at Chad in amazement. "What are you going to do now, bro?" Gus asked.

"Just get the money to Mr. P.," he replied. "This one's for him." He hit himself with the electric baton and fell to the floor next to Ferrell. He'd hurt himself to save my dad!

"Wow!" Gus said. And I agreed with him one hundred percent. Now the thing we had to do was get out of there — and fast!

Chapter 18

Austin

Maddy had really studied the bank. She knew exactly where to find a construction waste chute that we could ride straight out to the sidewalk beside the bank.

We rode it down like a big, turning amusement park tunnel slide. Max loved it, and I filmed him, laughing as he went around every turn. Finally, we burst out of a vent in the side of a wall into a construction Dumpster.

We scrambled out of the Dumpster feeling really excited and happy. We'd done it. Our go-carts were parked right there. All we had to do now was drive to the hospital and deliver the money.

But as I watched Gus climb out of the Dumpster behind me, I noticed something shiny dangling from his neck. It had come out from under his bandanna. "What is that?" I asked.

"What?"

"Around your neck," I said.

Gus was wearing a chain just like the one Maddy had given me! He felt for his bandanna and realized that it had come loose. He looked at Maddy and then at me. "Well, I guess we have something to tell you," he said.

He didn't need to tell me. I could pretty well figure it out for myself. But what he didn't know was that I had something to tell him, too.

I pulled off my bandanna and showed him my chain. We both whirled around and stared at Maddy angrily.

"We don't have time for this right now!" Maddy cried. "Let's go!"

She wasn't getting out of this that easily! *I* had the time! I couldn't think of anything that was more important at that moment. "I'm not going anywhere until I find out why Gus is wearing my chain," I shouted.

"Me, either," Gus agreed.

I turned back to Gus. "She played us."

"That sucks, Maddy," Gus said. "Let's get out of here, man," he said to me.

We didn't have to stick around to hear Maddy's explanation. What had happened was obvious.

"Right behind you," I told him. I can't remember ever feeling so mad at someone as I was at Maddy.

Gus and I got into our go-carts and drove off, leaving Maddy there holding Max.

While we drove, we talked to each other through the headsets built into our helmets. "Love hurts, huh?" I said to Gus.

"Tell me about it," he replied.

I noticed that my gas tank seemed low and mentioned it to Gus. He said I had enough to get back, but I wasn't so sure.

Then, from out of nowhere, we were surrounded by flashing lights and the sound of sirens. A sick feeling pushed up from the pit of my stomach.

On top of everything, Gus was wrong about my gas tank. The sputtering sound from my engine told me I was definitely running out of gas. "Gus . . ." I whimpered into my headset. "I don't want to be a juvenile delinquent." Above us, a police helicopter whirred. There would be no escaping this time.

"Pull your carts over immediately," a policeman's voice boomed from his car's speaker. Maybe Gus could outrun them, but I wasn't going anywhere in my dying go-cart.

The next thing I knew, Gus pulled alongside me. "Jump," he said, his voice coming over my headset.

"What?" I asked nervously.

"Jump into my cart!" he yelled.

This wasn't something I exactly knew how to do. I stood up in my cart, which was going slower every second. Standing in a moving go-cart isn't easy, and I didn't feel too steady.

"Come on. Do it!" Gus's voice boomed into my headset.

I can't believe I really did it — but I did it. I jumped into Gus's cart, letting my cart drive off by itself. The police sped up and drove right over my abandoned cart. They squashed it like a bug!

I crouched down behind Gus and saw the determined look in his eyes. He was not going to give up easily. Ahead of us, the police helicopter seemed to be landing. I had no idea how Gus planned to get away from *that*!

We kept racing toward the helicopter. For a second, I thought maybe Gus didn't see it or something. But he had to have seen it. There wasn't any way he could miss it! When we drove up to it, he hit the gas and shot directly under it.

It would have been a completely perfect maneuver except for one little thing. We crashed right into a fire hydrant when we came out from under the helicopter!

It knocked the bumper halfway off the front of the go-cart, but not completely off. The bumper dragged along on the outside of the cart, banging and smashing into the go-cart at every turn.

"Okay, buddy, hang on," Gus said.

"Why? What are we going to do?" I asked.

"I'm going to hit the X button," he said. I had no idea what the X button was, but it sounded cool. I knew Gus had been working on something special. He'd been hush-hush about it, though.

Gus hit the button!

I waited breathlessly.

Nothing happened.

He began pounding the dashboard. "Work, you piece of junk!" he shouted.

The go-cart started to slow down, and it seemed about to conk out. Some top-secret X button!

Furious, Gus slammed his hand on the dashboard. The go-cart suddenly sped up. The speedometer was whirring . . . 50 . . . 60 . . . 70 . . . 80 . . .

The police cars quickly fell farther and farther behind. By the time we screeched around a corner, I was pretty sure we'd lost them. Then, two police cruisers pulled out of an alley right in front of us.

"Hold on!" Gus cried as he pulled a hard right into the alley the police cars had just come out of. It was an alley filled with crates and barrels. Gus had no choice but to smash right through them. I felt as if we'd taken a turn and driven inside a video game.

As soon as we came out of the flying crates and barrels, I spied another police car right ahead of us. "Turn!" I yelled to Gus.

Gus did a hairpin turn into another alley. We seemed to have lost them. Both of us looked behind and saw no sign of them. But when we turned back, we were headed directly for an 18-wheel truck that had pulled into the intersection in front of us.

"Duck!" Gus shouted as he zoomed under the truck, clearing it by only inches.

We were in the clear! The police weren't around, and we didn't even hear the siren anymore. Gus and I high-fived. "Do you think Maddy made it?" he asked.

"I'm sure," I said. "I think the cops followed us, not her."

We looked at each other. We *weren't* sure she'd made it even though we were acting confident. "Gus," I began.

"Yeah?" he asked.

I didn't say anything because I was pretty sure he knew what I was thinking. We always seemed to think alike.

"We've got to go back, don't we?" he asked.

Chapter 19

Maddy

I steered my go-cart around the corner. Max was in my lap and he laughed, loving the ride. We were near the hospital. "Almost there, Max," I told him. Our mission was nearly complete.

I was in the middle of the intersection when suddenly three police cars came at me from three different directions. "Pull over! We have you covered!" an officer's voice blared over the car's intercom. "Pull over!"

Then, from out of the blue, Gus's go-cart

blasted into the intersection. The police cars swerved out of his way and got stuck in a ditch. They spun their wheels but they couldn't move.

Gus and Austin pulled alongside me and I smiled at them. I owed them big time for that one. The hospital was straight ahead. Side by side, we raced toward it.

Once we got there, we dashed up to Dad's room. Gus and Austin held on to Max and kept watch out in the hall. I ran into the room. "Dad! We're going to Denmark tonight for your operation," I told him. "I have the money." I cranked up the back of Dad's bed, preparing to wheel him out.

Outside, a police siren sounded. I couldn't panic though. It was important that I stayed calm and got Dad out of the hospital as quickly as I could.

"Maddy, what have you done?" Dad asked.

Before I could answer, Gus stuck his head into the room. "Maddy, we've got to go," he said urgently.

Mom, Alan Hartmann, and two police officers hurried into the room. "Madeline, what —" Mom began, but she cut herself short when she looked at me, then Dad. She must have suddenly understood what was going on. And, when she got it, her eyes began to fill with tears.

She wasn't the only one. Tears came to my eyes, too. They were tears of frustration and disappointment. I couldn't believe I'd gotten this far only to fail at the end.

"Molly, what's going on?" Alan asked me.

"I warned Mr. Brisbane that the security system wasn't online," Mom said to him.

"I know," Alan agreed.

"And to prove to everyone just how vulnerable the bank was . . ." Mom went on. She caught my eye and looked at me meaningfully. ". . . I had my daughter and her two friends — three kids — rob the bank."

I had new hope. Mom seemed to have a plan of her own.

"If you look in my contract," she continued, "you'll see that I have the license to perform undisclosed tests of the system until such date as the system is deemed fully operable."

"Are you buying this?" one of the officers asked Alan.

Alan looked at me and then he looked over my shoulder at Dad lying in his hospital bed. I could tell he was thinking, deciding what he wanted to do. I'd tricked him even though he'd been really nice to me. If he was mad at me, I could hardly blame him.

"Yeah, I buy it," he told the officer. "Molly Philips was authorized to bring in consultants to test the system. This was all a plan, a *brilliant* plan!"

I smiled at him, knowing that he realized it was all a big cover-up. He really was a great guy.

That night, Mom and I watched ourselves on the late-night news. A woman reporter stood in the right-hand corner of the TV screen and spoke to the audience. Behind her, you could see Mom and me leaving the hospital together.

"We understand that three children were involved in a high-speed pursuit ending here, at this hospital," she reported.

Using the remote, Mom switched channels. The story was on every network, too. "Details are sketchy, but it appears the children robbed the Lyons World Bank of nearly a quarter of a million dollars," the reporter on the next channel said. "A source inside the bank is saying the robbery was an elaborate plot to test the bank's security system."

"Good," Mom murmured. I guess she was glad to hear that this was how the story was being reported. She clicked to a local news channel. "Stories are swirling, but this reporter has found out that one of the children has a father who is in desperate need of an operation," the woman reporter said. "The child has not been identified, but her father is registered in the hospital as Tom Philips."

"They know about Dad," I said with a gasp.

Mom changed the channel again, and we discovered that another channel had picked up Dad's story. "Mr. Philips runs a local go-cart track and is scheduled to return home tomorrow, since insurance will not cover his operation."

I must have fallen asleep watching the TV. When I woke up, I was still on the couch with a blanket over me. Mom came into the living room, already dressed. She sat on the chair across from me. "You know that what you did was wrong, don't you, Madeline?" she asked.

I nodded. I'd done several things that I knew weren't right. Robbing the bank was only one of them. I also felt bad about lying to Alan, and even worse that I'd tricked Austin and Gus.

"I know I haven't been there for you — and that is going to change," Mom added. She hugged me. I started thinking about how she'd chosen my name as her code. It made me smile. She was a pretty terrific mom. "Let's go see Dad," she suggested.

Someone was pounding at our door. When I answered it, Austin and Gus were there. "You'd better come to the track," Gus said.

Mom and I stared at each other, bewildered. Austin and Gus had already hopped onto their bikes and headed out. So Mom and I climbed into the car and went down to the track.

When we were still over a block away, we could see that something was going on. Hundreds of people were lined up at the front gate.

Mom parked and we hurried to the front of the line. Gus, Chad, and Austin were already there. I saw that someone had broken the padlock off the front gate.

"What are all these people doing?" Mom asked the guys.

"They're waiting to buy tickets," Gus told her.

Mom used her keys to open the ticket desk,

and we started selling tickets. But people didn't want to pay the usual three-dollar entrance fee — they insisted on paying *more*!

One woman handed me a fifty and said, "Keep the change. Tell your dad to feel better."

The next kid gave me a fifty and told me to keep it. "It's from my parents," he said.

I couldn't believe it. After only an hour, the entire floor of the ticket desk was covered in money. All of us were counting as fast as we could.

Mom calculated the sum in a notebook. I glanced at her and my heart sank. She wasn't smiling and her eyes were sad as she looked up from her notebook at me. "Even with the donations through the news stations, we're still short," she said quietly.

Right then, Alan came to the ticket desk. "Molly," he said to Mom. "You forgot something."

Mom just stared at him. She seemed to have no idea what he was talking about. He handed a check to her. We all strained to see how much it was. Fifty thousand dollars!

"It's a consultant fee for the company you used to pull off the robbery," Alan explained. "That's you kids."

Austin, Gus, and I looked at one another, then high-fived one another. I couldn't believe we'd earned that much money.

"That should get you pretty close," Alan said. "And the president of the bank has authorized any necessary personal loan you might need."

That confused Mom. "But Brisbane . . ."

"Oh, I'm afraid he's not with the bank anymore," Alan told her. He straightened proudly. I got the definite impression that he had been promoted to president, and that Mr. Brisbane was now out of the picture.

It was amazing how fast Dad recovered from the operation he had in Denmark. It was really just a matter of months before he was back at the track and announcing the races. When I think about how close he came to not getting that operation, it gives me the shivers.

Things seemed to work out for everyone. Mom and I entered a whole new phase of our relationship. I now understood how important I really was to her. I think she saw a new side of me, too. Things were even looking good for Max, who said his second word — *Dada*. After that, there was no stopping him. The kid wouldn't shut up.

Gus and Austin forgave me for tricking them. But one major problem remained. They still wanted me to choose between them.

"Why do I have to choose?" I asked one afternoon as the three of us were walking up a grassy hill together.

"You can't have two boyfriends," Gus insisted. "Come on. Choose."

"Yeah, choose," Austin said at the same time.

Gus and Austin looked at each other like they always did when they said the same thing at the same time. Only this time they didn't glare at each other. They actually laughed. "Great minds think alike," Gus said.

Austin nodded. Then they both looked back at me. "Choose, Maddy," Austin repeated.

It was ridiculous. They wouldn't give up until I picked one of them. I had to do something.

"Okay," I agreed. I walked up to Gus and studied him. He was so cute and so sweet. Then I went over to Austin. He was so smart and so loyal. How could I ever pick? But I had to.

"All right," I told them. "I've made up my mind. Turn around."

They both turned, facing away from me. "No matter what happens, we'll be friends," Austin said to Gus. They had become friends, too. I never thought it would happen, but the robbery had turned them into true pals.

"Are you crazy?" Gus cried. "You're going to be the best man at our wedding."

Wedding? These two were way too serious for me. There was only one thing to do, and I did it. I began walking backward down the hill away from them. When I was far enough, I turned and ran.

They must have heard me because they turned, too. "Go get her!" Gus shouted.

"Maddy!" Austin cried. The two of them chased me down the hill. We were all laughing like crazy. I didn't know where it would end, but I was in no hurry to find out.